# *Alexander and the Wind-Up Mouse*

All rights reserved. Published in the United States by Dragonfly Books, an imprint of Random House Children's Books, a division of Penguin Random House LLC, New York. Originally published in hardcover in the United States by Pantheon Books, New York, in 1969.

Dragonfly Books with the colophon is a registered trademark of Penguin Random House LLC.

Visit us on the Web! rhcbooks.com

Educators and librarians, for a variety of teaching tools, visit us at RHTeachersLibrarians.com

The Library of Congress has cataloged the hardcover edition of this work as follows:
Lionni, Leo.
Alexander and the Wind-Up Mouse / by Leo Lionni.
p.   cm.
Summary: Alexander, the mouse, makes friends with Willy, a toy mouse, and wants to be just like him until he discovers that Willy is to be thrown away.
ISBN 978-0-394-80914-4 (trade) — ISBN 978-0-394-90914-1 (lib. bdg.)
[1. Mice—Stories.]
I. Title
PZ10.3.L6465 Al
76077423

ISBN 978-0-399-55551-0 (pbk.)

MANUFACTURED IN CHINA
January 2017
10

# Alexander and the Wind-Up Mouse

*by Leo Lionni*

*Dragonfly Books* ———→ *New York*

"Help! Help! A mouse!" There was a scream. Then a crash.
Cups, saucers, and spoons were flying in all directions.

Alexander ran for his hole as fast as his little legs would carry him.

All Alexander wanted was a few crumbs and yet
every time they saw him they would scream for help
or chase him with a broom.

One day, when there was no one in the house, Alexander heard a squeak in Annie's
room. He sneaked in and what did he see? Another mouse.
But not an ordinary mouse like himself. Instead of legs it had two little wheels,
and on its back there was a key.

"Who are you?" asked Alexander.

"I am Willy the wind-up mouse, Annie's favorite toy. They wind me to make me run around in circles, they cuddle me, and at night I sleep on a soft white pillow between the doll and a woolly teddy bear. Everyone loves me."

"They don't care much for me," said Alexander sadly. But he was happy to have found a friend. "Let's go to the kitchen and look for crumbs," he said.

"Oh, I can't," said Willy. "I can only move when they wind me. But I don't mind. Everybody loves me."

Alexander, too, came to love Willy. He went to visit him whenever he could. He told him of his adventures with brooms, flying saucers, and mousetraps. Willy talked about the penguin, the woolly bear, and mostly about Annie. The two friends spent many happy hours together.

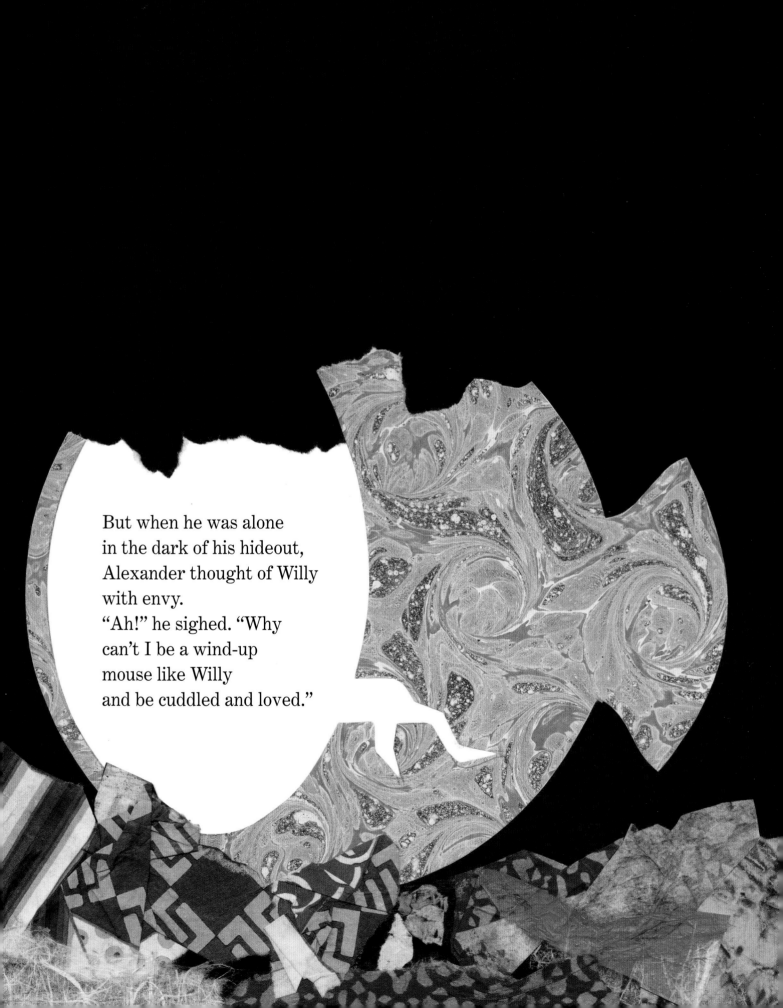

But when he was alone
in the dark of his hideout,
Alexander thought of Willy
with envy.
"Ah!" he sighed. "Why
can't I be a wind-up
mouse like Willy
and be cuddled and loved."

One day Willy told a strange story. "I've heard," he whispered mysteriously, "that in the garden, at the end of the pebblepath, close to the blackberry bush, there lives a magic lizard who can change one animal into another."

"Do you mean," said Alexander, "that he could change me into a wind-up mouse like you?"

That very afternoon Alexander went into the garden and ran to the end of
the path. "Lizard, lizard," he whispered. And suddenly there stood
before him, full of the colors of flowers and butterflies, a large lizard.
"Is it true that you could change me into a wind-up mouse?" asked Alexander
in a quivering voice.

"When the moon is round," said the lizard, "bring me a purple pebble."

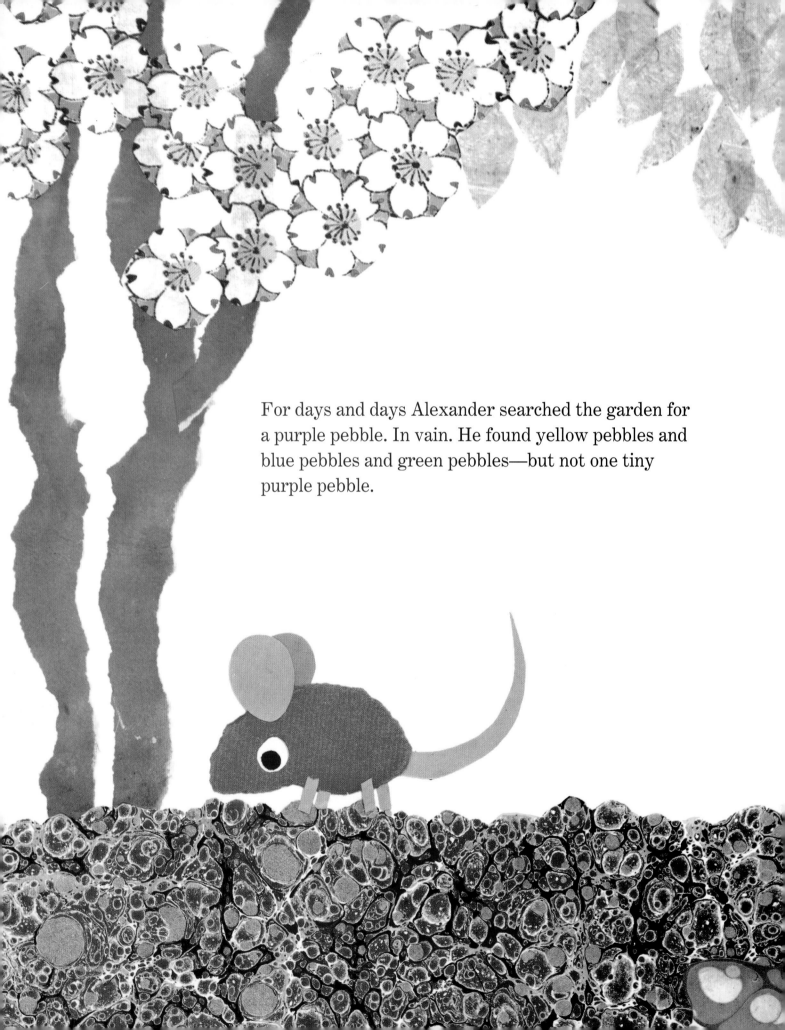

For days and days Alexander searched the garden for a purple pebble. In vain. He found yellow pebbles and blue pebbles and green pebbles—but not one tiny purple pebble.

At last, tired and hungry, he returned to the house. In a corner of the pantry he saw a box full of old toys, and there, between blocks and broken dolls, was Willy. "What happened?" said Alexander, surprised.

Willy told him a sad story. It had been Annie's birthday. There had been a party and everyone had brought a gift. "The next day," Willy sighed, "many of the old toys were dumped in this box. We will all be thrown away."

Alexander was almost in tears. "Poor, poor Willy!" he thought. But then suddenly something caught his eye. Could it really be . . . ? Yes it was! It was a little purple pebble.

All excited, he ran to the garden, the precious
pebble tight in his arms. There was a full moon.
Out of breath, Alexander stopped near the
blackberry bush. "Lizard, lizard, in the bush,"
he called quickly. The leaves rustled and
there stood the lizard. "The moon is round,
the pebble found," said the lizard. "Who or what
do you wish to be?"

"I want to be . . ." Alexander stopped.
Then suddenly he said, "Lizard, lizard,
could you change Willy into a mouse like me?"
The lizard blinked. There was a blinding
light. And then all was quiet. The purple pebble
was gone.

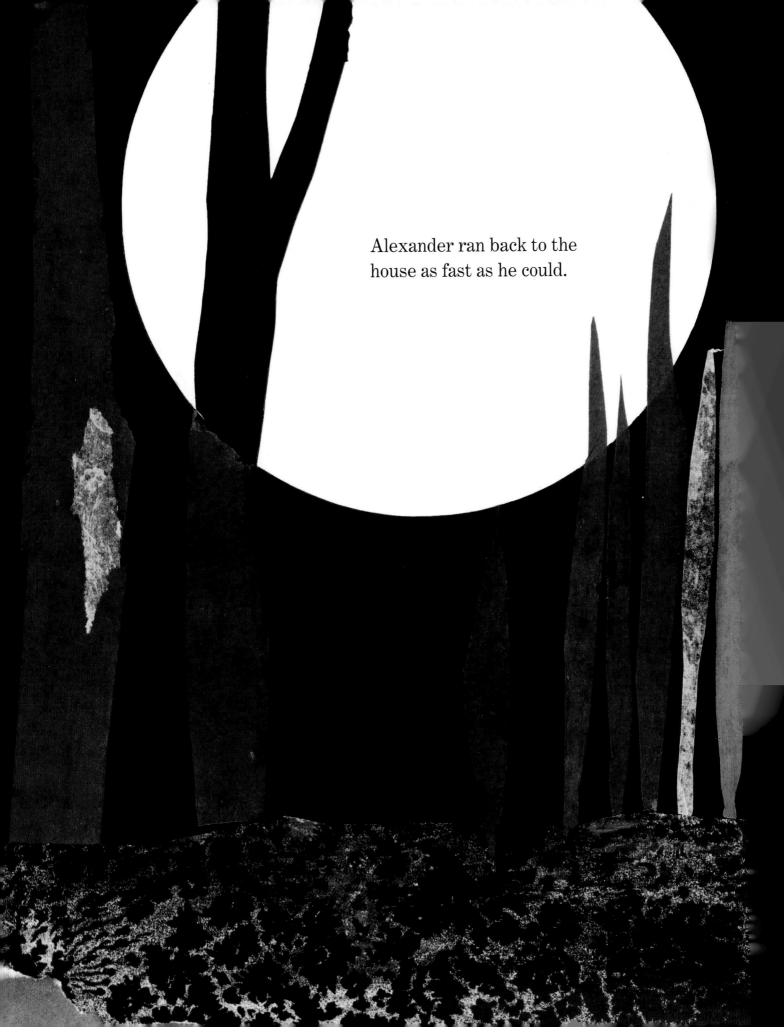

Alexander ran back to the house as fast as he could.

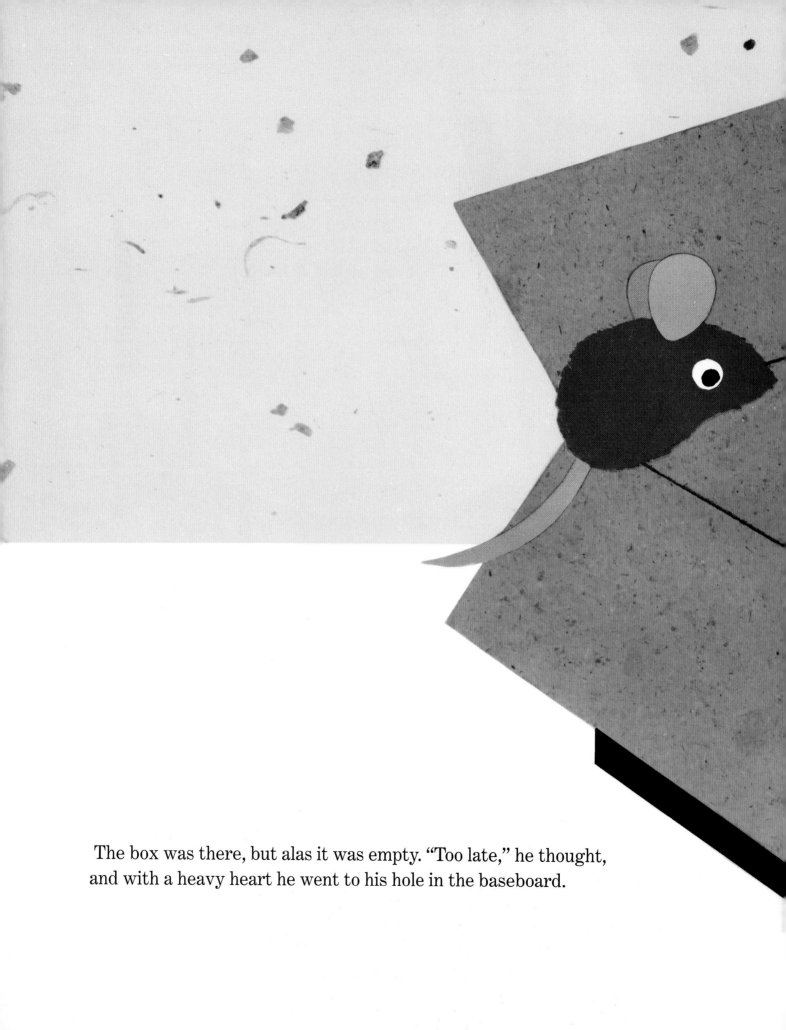

The box was there, but alas it was empty. "Too late," he thought,
and with a heavy heart he went to his hole in the baseboard.

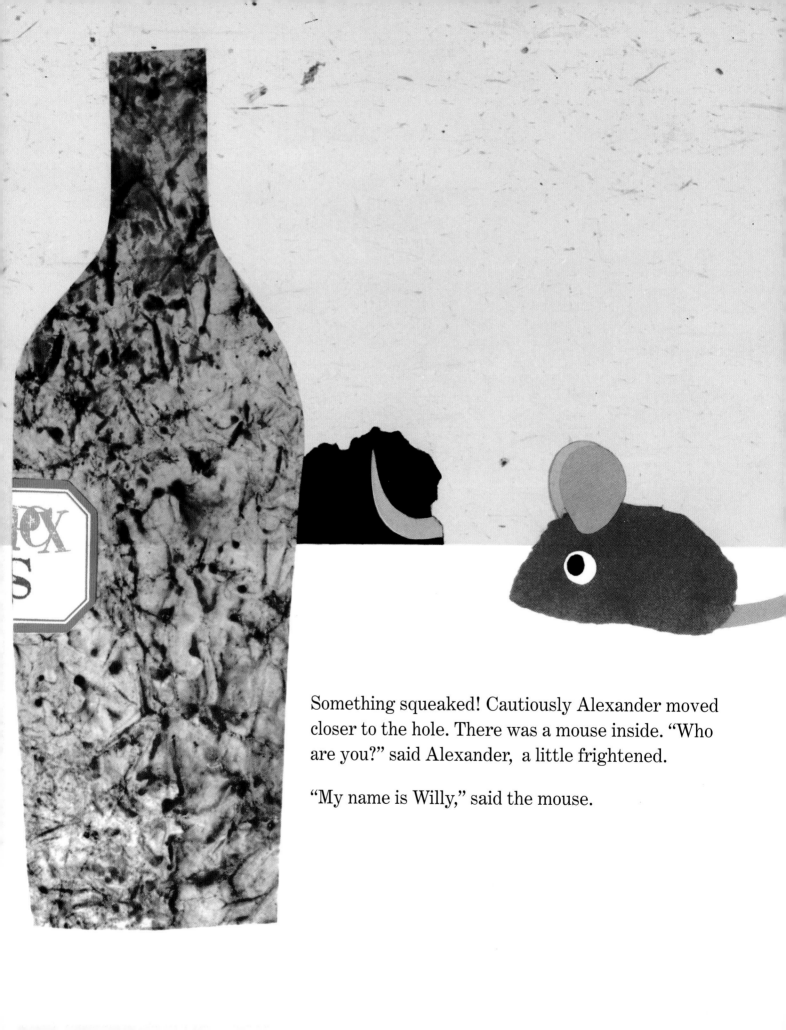

Something squeaked! Cautiously Alexander moved closer to the hole. There was a mouse inside. "Who are you?" said Alexander, a little frightened.

"My name is Willy," said the mouse.

"Willy!" cried Alexander. "The lizard . . . the lizard did it!"
He hugged Willy and then they ran to the garden path.
And there they danced until dawn.